Published by Magna Books
Magna Road
Wigston
Leicester LE18 4ZH

© 1994 Twin Books Ltd

Produced by TWIN BOOKS
Kimbolton House
117A Fulham Road
London SW3 6RL

Directed by CND – Muriel Nathan-Deiller
Illustrated by Van Gool-Lefèvre-Loiseaux

ISBN 1-85422-668-1

Printed in Slovenia

"'VAN GOOL'S'"

Ali Baba and the 40 thieves

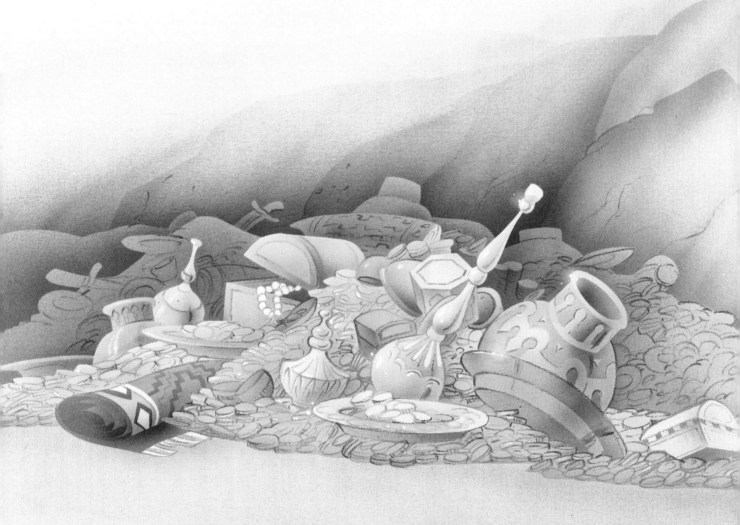

MAGNA BOOKS

Many years ago in Persia, there lived
a man called Ali Baba. He was a
humble woodcutter and hardly
earned enough money to live on.
One day he went to cut wood in the
forest. As he was tying his donkey to
a tree, he suddenly heard the clatter
of galloping hoofs approaching.

Curious to see who the horsemen were, he climbed up into a tall tree. He'd never seen so many men on horseback. He counted them. There were forty, all armed with weapons. "They look like ruffians," he muttered. "And what have they got in those big sacks? I'm sure they're thieves!"

The leader of the band got off his horse. He went over to a huge stone at the bottom of the hill, solemnly stretched out his arm and cried, "Open Sesame!"

Immediately the enormous stone
moved aside, revealing an opening in
the hillside. The thieves got off their
horses, picked up their sacks and
filed one by one into the cave.

Ali Baba was still in the
tree when they came out,
empty-handed. The leader
called, "Close, Sesame!"
and the rock moved back
into place as if nothing had
happened. Then the
robbers rode away.

"I must find out what is
in the cave," he thought.

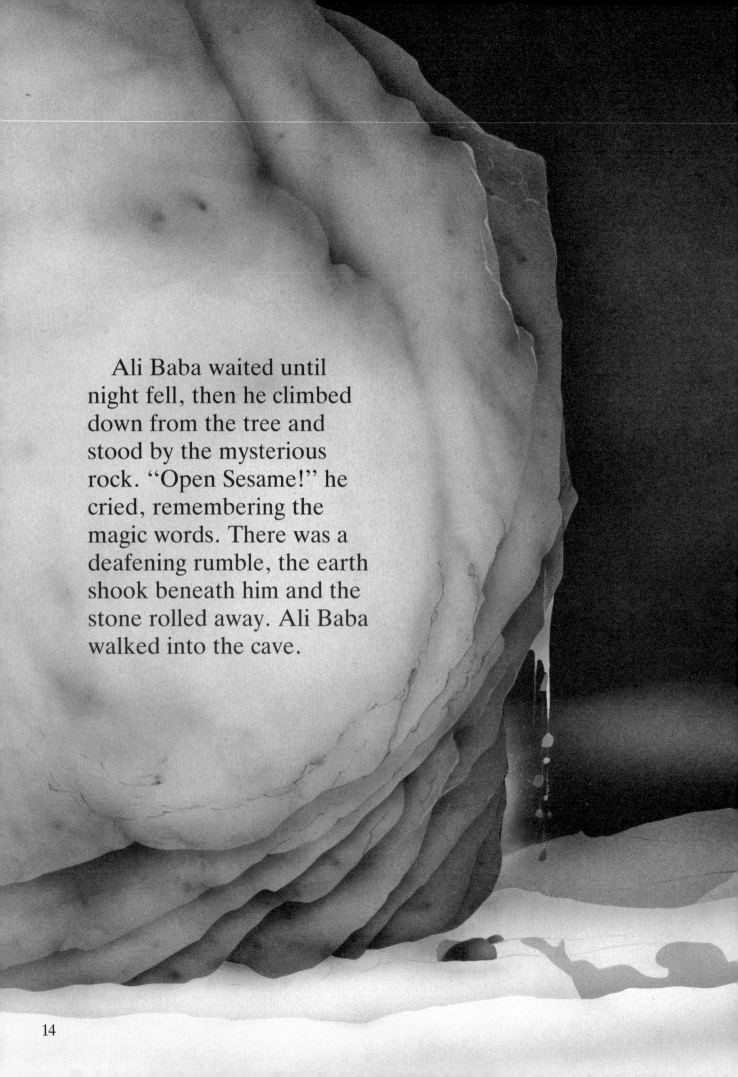

Ali Baba waited until night fell, then he climbed down from the tree and stood by the mysterious rock. "Open Sesame!" he cried, remembering the magic words. There was a deafening rumble, the earth shook beneath him and the stone rolled away. Ali Baba walked into the cave.

Inside he found just what he'd hoped for. There were jewels, piles of gold coins, beautiful rugs, carved wooden chests and wonderful swords with decorated scabbards.

It was a fantastic horde of treasure!

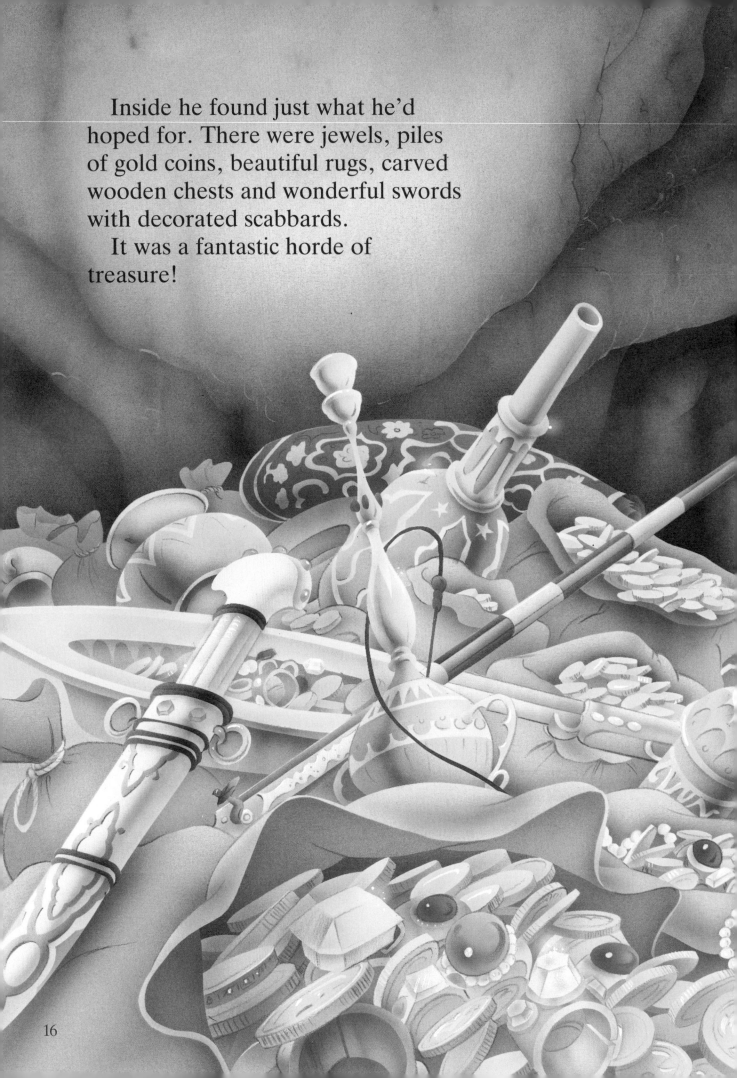

When his wife saw him come home with a sack of gold she was afraid he had stolen it.

"Fear not," said Ali Baba. "Stealing from thieves is not really stealing." He told her the whole story. "We're rich!" he exclaimed, and they rejoiced together.

Ali Baba's wife wanted to know exactly how rich they were. There was too much gold to count, so the next day she went to borrow a measure from Kassim, Ali Baba's rich brother, so that she could weigh the gold. Kassim's wife wondered what it was she wanted to measure, since Ali Baba was so poor. So before she lent her the measure she smeared a little glue in the bottom.

After the measure was returned, Kassim's wife saw a gold coin stuck to the bottom. "Look," she said to her husband jealously, "your brother is rich." Kassim was furious and went straight off to see Ali Baba.

22

"I know you're rich now," he said.
"But tell me, how did it happen?"
And Ali Baba, seeing that his
secret had been found out,
explained.

23

Ali Baba told his brother about the forty thieves and the riches piled up in the cave. He explained where the cave was and even told him the magic words! That very night, the greedy Kassim loaded ten donkeys with boxes and big sacks and led them quietly out of the village towards the forest.

Kassim found the rock easily and shouted, "Open Sesame!" The stone rolled away. He entered the cave and closed the entrance behind him. Planning to leave nothing for his brother, he gathered all the treasure, but when he tried to leave he'd forgotten the magic words.

"Open Rye! Open Corn!" he cried. "Open Barley!" But it was no use.

Suddenly the rock rolled aside and the band of thieves entered. Seeing the stranger amidst their treasure, the furious robbers rushed at him with their sabres drawn.

When Kassim didn't come back, his wife begged Ali Baba to help. Fearfully, Ali Baba rode his donkey to the cave. He found Kassim badly hurt by the thieves, who had left him for dead. He helped his brother onto the donkey and returned home.

Kassim's wife burst into tears when she saw her poor husband. Not trusting the town doctor to keep a secret, Ali Baba went to find Mustafa, the shoemaker.

"Will you sew up some sabre wounds?" he asked the old shoemaker, who was almost blind. "I'll pay you well, but you must tell no one."

"I promise," replied Mustafa.

And so Kassim's wounds were sewn together and began to heal. Kassim's wife and Ali Baba's servant Marjanah told all the villagers that Kassim was very ill, so no one was surprised not to see him. Kassim and his wife spent much time in Ali Baba's house until he was better.

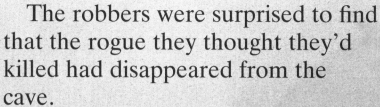

The robbers were surprised to find that the rogue they thought they'd killed had disappeared from the cave.

"Someone else knows our secret," declared the thieves' leader. He sent three of his men to the village to find out more. The thieves searched the streets looking for clues.

By chance, the three thieves met Mustafa, the shoemaker. "Ha, ha, ha!" they sniggered, "a blind cobbler!"

"It doesn't stop me sewing," said the old man. "Why, just last week I sewed up a man's wounds." He wasn't going to tell them any more, but a few gold coins soon persuaded him to talk.

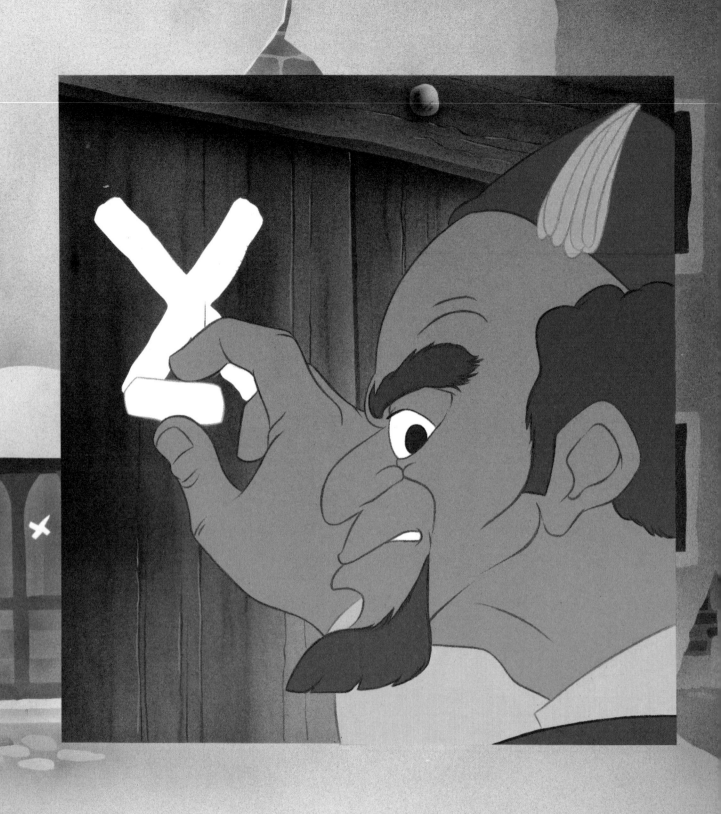

So the thieves found out where Ali Baba lived. One of them drew a cross on his door so they'd remember where it was. "Just you wait," he muttered. "Soon you'll be getting a visit."

The thieves didn't realise that the servant, Marjanah, had seen everything. As soon as it was dark she rushed out and drew a cross on all the other doors nearby.

41

The leader of the thieves came to town, but with all the doors marked with crosses he could not tell which house was Ali Baba's. He was furious.

The next day he went to see the shoemaker himself, taking a purse full of gold. Again Mustafa pointed out Ali Baba's house and said, "That's it."

The leader of the thieves took good note of it and then went to fetch his men.

The thieves worked out a crafty plan. The next day the leader arrived at Ali Baba's house with 39 horses carrying large jars.

"I'm a merchant," he said to Ali Baba. "My mules are exhausted from carrying these jars of oil which I plan to sell at the market tomorrow. And I'm tired too. Would you be kind enough to put me up for the night?"

"You are most welcome," said Ali Baba gladly.

The leader unloaded the
jars in Ali Baba's
courtyard. Then he joined
Ali Baba and his wife for
dinner. As Marjanah served
the meal, she stared at the
stranger suspiciously.

After dinner the leader went into the courtyard, pretending to check on his wares. But he was really checking on his men, for the jars contained not oil, but thieves armed with weapons!

In a low voice the leader said, "Wait quietly. In a little while I'll give you a signal and then you can attack!"

A little later the thieves heard
more footsteps in the courtyard. One
of them called out, "Is it time yet?"

Unfortunately for the thieves, it was Marjanah they'd heard. She'd come out for water from the well. She quickly guessed what was afoot and called out in a deep voice, "Not yet!" Then she went back into the kitchen.

Marjanah prepared a mixture of oils and spices that she knew would cause anyone who breathed the fumes to fall into a deep sleep. Then she crept back out to the courtyard and poured some into each jar in turn. The thieves fell asleep, one by one, without even time to shout out.

Marjanah's plan was not finished. Next she took her master to one side and asked if she might do some dances to entertain their guest. "Of course," replied Ali Baba, thinking it was a charming idea.

When everyone was seated, Marjanah began to sing and dance, delighting the bandit who stared at her in fascination. He had no idea what she was really planning to do.

Marjanah danced towards the thief. Suddenly she lunged at him, knocking him from his stool. Pulling his sabre from his belt, she held it against his heart. Marjanah made the thief believe she was a powerful sorceress who had cast a terrible spell on his men and on the cave of treasure. She showed the thief his sleeping men, then promised him that if he and his band would leave the country, she would remove the curse. Fearing for his life, he agreed.

The sleeping thieves awoke, and
fled after their terrified leader. Ali
Baba embraced Marjanah gratefully
and said, "Bless you, you have saved
my life."

The next day Ali Baba
waited until dark, then he
got onto his donkey and
rode quietly off to the cave.
The treasure was still there
and now it was all his.

Ali Baba shared his treasure with all his family and he didn't forget Marjanah either. He gave her enough money to live like a queen, but she was loyal to her master and chose to stay with him. Ali Baba was touched by this and treated her as his own daughter for ever afterwards.